# THE WOLF
## WHO DIDN'T LIKE TO DISCARD
# Read

By Orianne Lallemand
Illustrations by Éléonore Thuillier

**AUZOU**

There once was a wolf whose appetite for books was insatiable.
Big books and small, fairy tales or dictionaries… He ate them all!
He couldn't help himself.
He simply loved the taste of paper.

His name was Wolf.

"But don't you want to read the stories?" an annoyed Wolfette asked him. "Books are full of adventure and excitement!"

"I prefer real adventures!" Wolf replied. "Reading is boring…"

"Really?" said Owl. "I bet *this* book won't bore you. We chose it just for you."

"And we won't play with you again until you've read it!" added Wolf's friend, Alex.

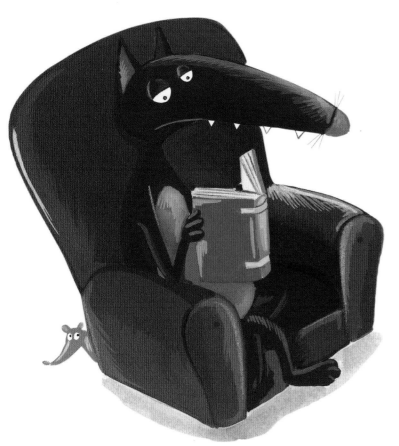

Back home, Wolf settled into his chair. Feeling grumpy, he opened the book and turned a page, then two...

After the third page, Wolf fell asleep.

Wolf heard someone crying.
He looked around. Wolf was no longer in his room.
He was in a forest filled with books!

At the foot of a tree, a squirrel was moaning.
"Where did I put them? I have no idea where
I put them…"

"Where did you put what?"
Wolf asked, politely.

"My books! Ten of my books have
disappeared!"

7

Wolf rubbed his eyes, I must be dreaming, he thought.
"Who are you? And, where am I?" Wolf asked the squirrel.

"I'm the librarian," replied the squirrel.
"And you are in the main library in Book World.
Here, we keep a copy of every book ever written.
But ten of the books are missing!"

"I can help you look for them, if you'd like?" Wolf offered.

"Oh my, yes. Thank you!" the squirrel replied. "If you find them, could you please put them in this bag?"

Delighted by the idea of an outing, Wolf sauntered away. His stroll was soon halted by the sharp cry of a crow perched in a tree. On the grass below the tree, a fox stood laughing. "Hmm, I feel like I've seen this before, but where?" Wolf mused.

"Yesterday, you stole my cheese!" screeched the crow. "And now you steal my book!"

"This isn't your book, it is mine!" countered the fox as he slipped it into his basket.

While the fox and crow argued, Wolf seized the book. "There, one book found!" Wolf chuckled as he walked toward a shady spot.

Wolf sat on the ground under a tree. He was *so* hungry, and the book looked delicious. He only wanted a little taste. Mid-bite, Wolf was startled by a white rabbit, mumbling as he hurried by.

"Oh dear! Oh dear! I shall be too late!"

A book under one arm, the rabbit was waving his watch when he disappeared as quickly as he'd appeared.

Without a second's hesitation, Wolf followed the rabbit down a long tunnel. The delicious scent of toast, butter, and vanilla cream cakes filled the air.

"Welcome to Wonderland," said the white rabbit. "Why are you here?"

Wolf looked at the party of odd characters seated around a large table. "I'm looking for the books the librarian lost. You seem to have…"

"This one?" smiled rabbit, handing the book to Wolf. "It's about Alice… and me. It's very exciting!"

"And in return, you will join us for tea," said the Cheshire Cat, smiling his toothy grin.

"That makes two!" Wolf said as he placed the book into his bag. Then he sat down for a bit of tea.

" **MMMM!** This all tastes so good!"

Having finished his tea, Wolf said his good-byes, and walked out the door... only to find himself in a jungle!

He had only taken a few steps when he saw two books lying on a rock. Wolf was a little disappointed that they were so easy to find.

"Two plus one makes three, and one more is four," said Wolf, adding the books to his bag.

Wolf heard something rustling in the trees just as a boy riding a black panther shot out like a rocket!

"If I were you, I wouldn't stand there," the boy cried. "Shere Khan, the tiger is coming!"

Suddenly, a tremendous roar rumbled through the air.
Petrified, Wolf froze.

**RRRRRRRRR!**

"Quick, climb this tree!"
ordered a voice from above.

Wolf didn't need to think twice;
he scaled that tree, fast!

Someone was waiting at the top.

"Who are you?" asked Wolf.

"I'm Peter Pan, and you are Wolf!" said the boy. "You seem to have a knack for showing up where you shouldn't, but there's no time to chat. We can't stay here; Captain Hook is after me! Come, I'll take you to Neverland."

Peter sprinkled a pinch of fairy dust on Wolf and soon they were flying! Sadly, their landing didn't go so well. They tumbled to the ground just as a huge net fell over them.

"Finally, I have caught you, Peter Pan!" crowed Captain Hook.

"And who is that with you? Well, shiver me timbers, it's a wolf!"

"Release us, Hook," admonished Peter. "Wolf doesn't belong here. He's not part of our story!"

"Your friends are me enemies," replied Hook. "Guards, grab these landlubbers and lock 'em up!"

Locked in a cabin on the pirate's ship, Wolf yawned.
"All these adventures are wearing me out. I need a nap."
Reclining on the bed, Wolf had started to fluff the pillow
when he discovered two books hidden beneath it.
The first was *Treasure Island*. "Now, I've found five books!"
The second one had a picture of a submarine being attacked
by a giant octopus.
"Make that six," said Wolf.

Wolf timidly opened the second book
and read the title, *Twenty Thousand
Leagues Under the Sea*. Hmm, he wondered, what's this about?
That's when he heard a terrible **CRAAACKK**,
and the pirate ship began to fill with water.
Wolf panicked, but managed to escape through a window.
Once he was in the water, he remembered something important.
He couldn't swim!

"Help! I'm going to drown!" Wolf cried,
closing his eyes as he fell through the water.
Just then, an enormous shark swooped down
and swallowed him in one gulp!
Wolf cautiously opened his eyes, only to find himself
inside Ali Baba's cave!

Sifting through the treasure piled on the cave floor, Wolf found four more books: *Aladdin*, *The Adventures of Robin Hood*, *Ali Baba and the Forty Thieves*, and *Sinbad the Sailor*.

"Six books, plus one makes seven. One more is eight, and one more makes nine.  Add in the last one, and I have ten! Ten books!" Wolf was delighted.
"Mission accomplished! Now, how do I get out of here?"

"I'm afraid you're stuck here, just like us," said the puppet who'd been hiding in a corner.
"But my father, Geppetto, has an idea. If we start a fire, the smoke might make the shark sneeze. Then, while his mouth is open, we can escape! Do you want to help?"

Wolf, and the puppet named Pinocchio, gathered a large pile of wood. Then Geppetto set the wood on fire. Soon the inside of the shark was full of smoke and...

## AHH... AHH... AAH... AAAAAAAACHOOOOOOO!

The shark sneezed so hard it sent them flying, clinging to the carpet!

When the carpet finally stopped, Wolf was shaken, but amazed. He had landed in the middle of the library!

"Ah, is that you, Wolf?" asked the librarian, relieved. "I was wondering where you were."

"Here are your books," answered Wolf. "I found them all!"

"Astounding! Thank you. You are truly a librarian's best friend!" replied the squirrel.

As the librarian returned each book to its shelf, Wolf heard what sounded like a big sigh. It was the pages of the books closing with a soft **PFFFF...**

Wolf woke to find himself in his chair.
In his lap was the book his friends had given him.
He grabbed it excitedly. Wolf was full of questions!
Where was Wonderland?
Who was that boy riding the panther in the jungle?
Had Peter Pan escaped from the villain, Captain Hook?

Wolf was so absorbed in his reading
that he didn't hear his friends enter.

"Hey Wolf, come outside and play
with us!" called Alex.

"Maybe later," answered Wolf.
"Right now, I'm busy reading."

In this adventure, Wolf found the following books:
- *Aesop's Fables*
- *Alice's Adventures in Wonderland*, by Lewis Carroll
- *Tarzan of the Apes*, by Edgar Rice Burroughs
- *The Jungle Book*, by Rudyard Kipling
- *Treasure Island*, by Robert Louis Stevenson
- *Twenty Thousand Leagues Under the Sea*, by Jules Verne
- *The Adventures of Robin Hood*, by Howard Pyle
- *Aladdin and the Enchanted Lamp*, from *The Arabian Nights*
- *Ali Baba and the Forty Thieves*, from *The Arabian Nights*
- *The Seven Voyages of Sinbad the Sailor*, from *The Arabian Nights*

And he also met characters from these books:
- *Peter Pan*, by J. M. Barrie
- *The Adventures of Pinocchio*, by Carlo Collodi

Managing Director: Gauthier Auzou
Senior Editor: Agathe Lème-Michau
Editor: Marie Marin
Cover Design: Alice Vignaux
Graphic Design: Eloïse Jensen
Production Manager: Jean-Christophe Collett
Production: Bertrand Podetti
Project Management for the present edition: Ariane Laine-Forrest
Translation from French: MaryChris Bradley

Printed and made in China, May 2018
ISBN: 978-2-7338-5619-2

    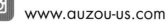 www.auzou-us.com

# WHO'S AFRAID OF THE BIG BAD WOLF?

Meet Wolf! His quirky, tongue-in-cheek humor, and fun-loving personality is perfect for children. His lively adventures will appeal to early readers and parents alike.

Wolf is now a household name in France thanks to the fundamental concepts—such as accepting yourself, birthdays, and history—subtly woven into each story. Welcome Wolf into your home too!

*Being naughty has never been so good!*

*In the same series:*

     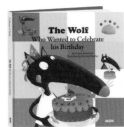

*Also available:*